DOWN-AND -OUT

Other Orchard Storybooks

A CLIPPER STREET STORY

DOWN-AND
-OUT

Bernard Ashley

Illustrated by
Jane Cope

ORCHARD BOOKS
London

Text copyright © Bernard Ashley 1988
Illustrations copyright © Jane Cope 1988
First published in Great Britain in 1988 by
ORCHARD BOOKS
10 Golden Square, London W1R 3AF
Orchard Books Australia
14 Mars Road, Lane Cove NSW 2066
Orchard Books Canada
20 Torbay Road, Markham, Ontario 23P 1G6
1 85213 077 6
Typeset in Great Britain by Tradespools Ltd,
Station Road, Frome, Somerset
Printed in Great Britain by A. Wheaton, Exeter

The Clipper Street stories are set
in and around the Greenwich area
of South East London which is
shown on the map overleaf.

CHAPTER ONE

You don't lie-in a lot when you're old. Not unless you're ill. Even then, you're best off getting up and getting going if you can. Because lying there thinking about things doesn't make you smile too much.

So Mrs Powell was always up and doing by seven whether it was Sunday, Monday or Christmas—spreading her jobs as thin as butter to make them last the day. Which is why she spent such a lot of time at her window, watching Clipper Street go by.

In the mornings—with her overall on— she would stand in her front room with her second cup of tea, watching for certain faces. Like little Roberta from next door—pretty little girl with the serious look, but always a smile when she waved. And that little tough-nut with the football from over the road. She'd like to tell his mum a thing or two about boys showing off—because he toed the line with a *please* and a *thank you* when his ball came over here! And the young woman—bit of a girl—from number seven who went to work in some new creation every day. Like a fashion plate, she was, toddling for the train. And her hair . . . !

But it was all go for half an hour, and that suited Nellie Powell. A wave to her at her window was worth a fiver, she reckoned. Made the rest of the day go a bit quicker.

This morning she put on her pink overall for a change. She wouldn't want people to think she only ever wore the one, dirty thing. She refilled her cup to the brim and went into the front room to sip it slowly. She thought the windows might do with a wipe, later on. Perhaps give those net curtains a rinse.

And that was the end of passing thoughts. She looked out—and she looked again. Because there was someone on her wall, sitting on her coping like Lord Muck. Someone in an old overcoat with the collar turned up. Well, of all the blessed cheek . . . .

Nellie rattled down her cup and rapped on her window. It was a hard knock with a hard old knuckle, enough to make the frame rattle and the man look round.

And when he did, she knew exactly what he was. A down-and-out from the doss house. And, typical! With a newspaper under his backside and a bottle in his hand.

"Go on!" she shouted. "Clear off! You're not parking there all day!" She waved her hand at him as if he were a dog. "Sling your hook, go on, get off with you!"

But the man took no notice. He wiped the top of the bottle with his palm, put it back on the pavement and stared at it.

"I'm not having this!" Nellie said. And in a surge of anger — with just the smallest ripple of fear — she hurried for the door.

CHAPTER
TWO

If she'd thought the banging of the woodwork would have him off, she was wrong. Still he sat there. She put a mat in the door and came right out to him. But he went on staring at the pavement even as she tapped his shoulder.

"You can't sit there, you know. This is a private wall, not council. You can't sit there all day." That's what Nellie really feared. Not someone just taking the weight off their feet. She'd lived in the district all her life. She knew the down-and-out routine. She saw it every time the bus took her through Deptford High Street.

The hostel threw them all out at eight in

the morning, and they weren't allowed back in till eight at night. *Move on*, was the message. Move on to the next one. Don't make a home here. But most of them went no further than the nearest wall. Or they sat in local doorways all day. They drank what they could lay their hands on, they argued,

and they fought. A disgrace, they were. And here was one who'd wandered right off the beaten track and ended up sitting in a decent street . . . .

"Are you deaf? Did you hear me? Get off of there!"

The man hadn't moved and he didn't

answer. He just sat there dangling the bottle between his knees. Now she could see that it was cider.

"You can move, mate, or I'll fetch a policeman," she told him. "Because you're not staying there...." Nellie looked helplessly up and down the street. But there was no one in sight: no one on the move when you wanted them.

"I've got the telephone," she said. "And I'll use it. Nine-nine-nine! See if I don't...."

But still there was no move, if you didn't count a big sigh.

"Don't know what's brought you round here. Your sort aren't supposed to get this far...."

Now there was a cough, and the head turning. And one thin hand came off the bottle to wave at the half-dozen roses in Nellie's front garden.

"Come to smell the flowers, ma'am," the man said. And he looked up at Nellie: a tired face, a few days' stubble and none too clean.

But with eyes of a willow pattern blue: and so very young and clear.

It took away Nellie's next breath.

"But you're only . . . a boy . . . ." she said. "You're . . . ."

He smiled at her; no gaps in his teeth, either. "You don't have to be old to be on the skids, ma'am. Nor to have a fancy for the smell of flowers." He nodded his head, more to himself than to her, and took another small swig from his bottle. "Bad things nor good, they're not reserved for the elderly." He wiped his mouth with the sleeve of his coat and went back to staring at the pavement. "Indeed they're not, ma'am."

CHAPTER
THREE

It took a lot to shock Nellie Powell these days. What with the things you saw on the telly, and what her son-in-law told her. But this young man had really got her lost for words. He was polite, he spoke nicely, just a bit of Irish in him. And he was so *young* to be down-and-out. His hair was dirty: well, more dusty: but it wasn't all long and freakish.

And his eyes were alive, like . . . like . . . .

She half-turned to go. She wanted rid of *that* thought. Let him stay where he was. She'd draw her curtains. She didn't have to see him. After all, he'd go in his own good time, when the bottle ran out, wouldn't he?

But her feet wouldn't move her. She

couldn't go. And that thought refused to go, too. Yes, his eyes were a lot like her Paul's, when her Paul had been telling her something serious. The colour, the shape, the shine that always looked like the start of a cry . . . .

"That stuff'll do you no good," she told the young man. "Rot your guts."

She looked him up and down as if deciding something. But the decision had been made as soon as she'd seen those eyes.

"How would you like a nice cup of tea for a change? Like your mother makes?"

A handbell rang in the school playground. A ship's hooter sounded on the river. The roar of heavy lorries round the one-way system gave a constant background. But all Nellie heard was the young man answering.

"Thank you very much, ma'am. Thank you very much." His arm seemed to be going for another swig, but he set the bottle down. "I'd like it fine."

"Right you are, then. You sit there and

smell the flowers." Nellie's legs were pre-
pared to obey her now. "I'll freshen up the
pot."

But she hadn't got far, back along the path,
when she saw someone coming across the
road like Securicor. It was the man with the
beard, Mr Roberts, the sportsman from

number twelve. The boy on the wall watched him coming, too—the jeans, trainers, sweat shirt and meaty arms.

"This guy giving you any hassle, is he?" Sam Roberts had the sort of voice fifty press-ups before breakfast develop.

The down-and-out was back staring at the pavement. It's not often people hit someone who isn't looking.

"Oh, thank you very much, Mr Roberts. But he's all right. He's going to have a cup of tea and then he's going."

"*Scrounging* a cup of tea, is he?"

"Oh, no . . . I'm offering." Nellie wondered why she had to sound sorry for doing such a thing.

"Long as you know what you're about."

"I think so." Nellie smiled sweetly and watched him go. Down to the shop for his paper: then back across indoors, to keep an eye, no doubt.

And why not? she thought. What *was* she doing? She didn't know this boy from Adam.

What on earth had come over her? She'd gone out there to chase him off and here she was brewing up for him.

Was it really all over a pair of eyes which stupidly put her in mind of her Paul. . . ?

CHAPTER
FOUR

But her regrets and her mixed-up feelings soon flew away when she saw how he enjoyed his tea. His eyes closed as he sipped: and he didn't wipe his mouth on his sleeve now, he did it neatly with a thumb. It was as if only part of his life was hostel behaviour.

"That's a treat, ma'am, that's a real treat," he said. "I haven't had a real cup of tea like that since I don't know when."

He stood up and handed her the cup and saucer, gave a little bow. And as if there were a correct way of doing that, too, he folded the newspaper he'd been sitting on and put it away in a pocket.

"Thank you for that, ma'am, and thank you

for the smell of the flowers."

He smiled, his eyes smiling, too. And Nellie Powell suddenly found her heart thumping up tight in her throat. What was a boy like this—a boy no older than her Paul had been—what was he doing leading the life of a down-and-out?

If her heart was in her throat then it was her heart which was suddenly speaking.

"Well, if you like flowers so much, how

would you like to . . . earn a few coppers . . . looking to some? I tell you, I've got more on my plate than I can cope with out the back."

Heavens! Was that her talking? Had she asked him in? This perfect stranger, a scruffy young man who could *murder* her? She shot a look across the road to see if the sportsman's curtains twitched. But she saw nothing. And now she heard nothing but this business going one step further.

"I'd like that very much, ma'am, thank you."

And she was delighted. Overjoyed.

"Come on, then," she said. "Mind, I haven't got much in the way of tools. But a pair of strong young arms should make up for that . . . ."

He pocketed his cider. He slid it down into a side pocket with the ease of a lord casing his binoculars. And then, from some other life, he flattened his hair with his hands as if he'd just removed his hat, and he entered her house.

CHAPTER
FIVE

She took him straight through. He seemed to be bigger, inside: perhaps because most other people inside her house were only television screen size. He seemed to fill the living room doorway. She heard his bottle clunk on the woodwork.

"Through here," she said, hurrying. She didn't want to look at his face. She would have hated seeing his eyes dart about at her little treasures. "It's mostly grass, for easiness. That needs a cut, too. But it's the beds could do with a good weeding."

In fact, neither flowers nor grass needed much doing to them. She enjoyed kneeling on her mat at the flowers, and only last week she'd run her electric mower over the lawn. But what else could she have asked him to do? She couldn't have him *indoors*, could she?

She found him a spade and he started work in his overcoat. Like a farm labourer, she thought. But the sun got up a bit, and when she next looked out—when *wasn't* she looking out?—he'd hung it on the cleat to the clothes line.

And she swallowed when she saw his clothes. He was wearing a short jumper full of holes, nothing under it, no shirt or vest. And a pair of trousers too long, held up with a length of flex. As for shoes, they were women's plastic boots and sizes too small. With no socks, neither. Poor little devil. . . !

It was clear that he had very little idea of what he was doing. His method of weeding was to lift a spade full of earth onto the grass and root around in it for anything green. Dig, toss, root; dig, toss, root. He worked fast and furious, but there was no

real order to what he did. One minute he was this side of the garden, the next over there. And one thing was very sure. The place was going to look the worse for his attention, not better.

She went out to him.

"Oh, you are getting on well."

Well, the gardening wasn't the point. It was just a job. He could have dug holes then filled them in as far as she was concerned.

"Now, what would you say to a nice bit of dinner later on? Boiled ham. And then banana custard?"

Stupid old woman! she thought. Not for the question—but for her heart which was beating like a little bird's till those eyes looked at her and said yes.

"I'd like that fine, ma'am, an' thank you very much."

He turned back to his work with the air of someone too busy to talk.

Nellie watched her garden being ruined, and she smiled. She even put a hankie to her eye as she went indoors to peel two extra potatoes. It was lovely to have someone to cook for again. Someone with a young man's appetite . . . .

CHAPTER
SIX

They sat at a card table she put up in the kitchen. Well, she wasn't going to insult him with a cooked meal served up in the garden. But at the same time, she wasn't too happy about having him in the living room. Not till she knew his name, at least.

"It's William, ma'am," he told her. "Properly. They all make it Bill, on the street. But being Irish it should be Liam if they're goin' to shorten it."

Nellie nodded, and thought about Paul: how she'd picked a name no one could alter. And she watched this young man eat. Saw how he ate his food politely, but fast, and left some—as if it wasn't food he wanted so much as something else . . . .

"What are you doing in England, then, William?"

"Not a lot, ma'am. Nothin', you'd say."

"I mean, why come across? With no work to go to?"

"Because there's no work *there*, ma'am, neither."

"And no family? No one to turn to?"

"No ma'am. I never had that privilege." And he smiled at her shyly, held her eyes for a second before looking back at his plate.

So he was all alone and down-and-out in London. All set on a slippery slope which could only lead him further down.

She looked at the rough face from which shone the eyes of a boy. Couldn't someone help a young man like this?

"An' you, ma'am: on your own, are you?"

To her shame, Nellie Powell didn't answer at once. Might he knock her over the head if she said yes too quickly?

"Yes, I'm all alone now," she told him. She stood to get the custard. "My husband's been dead for more years than ever I knew him. But I've got a daughter near, and a son-in-law...." And here she stopped. She always had to compose herself for this next bit.

William sat quietly, while a banana was sliced into his custard. Again, he kept his eyes on his plate, as life had taught him.

"I had a son. Paul. But he died in a war everybody's forgot. A war they don't even make films about."

She stood on the waste bin pedal and flopped the banana skin into it. And, saying no more, she sat to watch her young down-and-out eat his banana custard.

William cleared his plate, said something about getting on, and went out again into the garden.

CHAPTER
SEVEN

Nellie's usual routine after lunch was to wash up and have ten minutes in her armchair. Then, in good time to see the kiddies coming home from school, she'd splash her face at the sink and put on an afternoon dress. A fresh cup of tea and she'd be at her front window again.

Today was different, though. Today, while she could hear the homely sound of spade hitting flint in the garden, she went upstairs to the spare bedroom.

It was small and at the back of the house. From the window she could see William working. Actually, it was starting to look a little bit better down there, she thought. He was getting things straighter. But that wasn't what she was looking for. It was his coat hanging up that she concentrated on. The coat with the cider bottle still in the pocket. Because she could see that while he'd been working there, while he'd had something to do, he hadn't needed even to slake his thirst.

And that being the case, she could look round the room for a reason.

All the room did was sit here and hold spare furniture. It was never used. Her daughter lived too near to stay. And, sad to say, there weren't any grandchildren to come for a night at their nan's. She'd often thought about letting it—taking in a girl student, or a young businesswoman. But then she'd see that creature up the road with the hair and somehow she'd always go off the idea.

But giving a decent bed to a young boy in need .... Well, that was different, wasn't it? That was like the Good Samaritan.

She re-arranged the room in her mind.

41

Became excited about her plan. She could tell herself she was doing it for . . . . Sort of, do as you would be done by . . . .

Like everyone on a high, though, she had to come down. What if William wouldn't accept? What if it wasn't what he wanted? Some birds hate to be caged. Some people, too. For some people, drifting about is the only life they want. They call it Freedom, and perhaps William was one of those.

Well, there was only one way to find out. She'd make up the bed and let him see it, all comfortable-looking. She'd move what furniture she could to make the place look like a bedroom again. And then she'd ask him if he wanted to stay. It *had* to be better than some hostel, she told herself.

Mind, she wouldn't be stupid over it. She'd say it was just for the one night. Then if things went wrong in some way, if they didn't work out, he could go off in the morning with no hurt feelings. And she'd let him know she was telling her daughter what she was doing: for safety.

Yes, that's what she would do.

On the wall of the room was a little motto. She'd had it for years. Now she looked at it again, read its meaning.

We shall never get giddy by the good turns we do.

Well, she didn't get much chance to do good turns. But here was one, wasn't there? All some people needed in life was a leg up when they were down. Someone to give them a hand. All right, then! she thought. Now was her chance to do just that.

She looked out of the window again. William was still going at it. He hadn't paused, didn't mind hard work. Now he was trimming the lawn with a pair of shears he'd found in the shed.

Nellie leant an old, veined hand on the window ledge and watched him. Her eyes filled again with tears. Poor kid. Poor little Irish kid, so far from home. Could be anyone's son or grandson, working out there.

Just a chance was all he needed. And a little bit of love.

On an impulse she raised the window and leaned out.

"Time for a cup of tea, William?"

He stopped his clipping, looked up at her and waved.

"Thank you, ma'am. That'll be very nice."

"Then put the kettle on, would you? You know where it is. And it's *Nellie*, not *Ma'am*."

"Right you are, Nellie. Thank you." And, rubbing his red hands, in he went to put on the kettle for their tea.

CHAPTER
EIGHT

Nellie was halfway down the stairs when she stopped and had her second thoughts. They always come: what matters is *when*. She paused by a picture of her husband, a careful studio portrait she'd made him have done.

It was the afternoon light, no doubt, but wasn't it almost as if he were shaking his head? He had always been a cautious man. She had once caught him checking the length of one ruler in his tool box against another. He always had two thermometers in his greenhouse. He was a person who could lay his hands on the spare buttons which came with a new suit, months after. Now he seemed to be staring at Nellie, very straight.

Giving a room to a perfect stranger? his eyes asked. And a down-and-out at that? He could ransack the house in the night, murder you in your bed! Have you forgotten some of the dreadful things which happen to old people? There's no bolt on your bedroom door and no time to fit one, either . . . .

Nellie dusted the glass of the picture with her sleeve. She was sure young William could be trusted. If he'd meant her harm he'd had every chance to do it during the day. He could have knocked her on the head and gone off with anything by now.

No, clear blue eyes like that don't lie. She knew those eyes of old, every mood in them. And there was no danger in this boy. No danger at all.

Nellie was gripping the banister rail hard. Now she turned and went back up the stairs again. Stupid old woman! She was getting in a proper state over this. At her age she could cope with just about everything except not making up her mind.

She went back to the small bedroom. She looked out yet again, this time making sure not to be seen.

William was crouching down on the grass like little boys do, playing with next door's cat. Tickling it; so gentle . . . .

Standing back, she eyed the distance between this room and hers, along the landing. Six or seven big steps separated the doors. Just a few seconds in time if someone was hurrying.

Like a little old lady in a fairy story she

turned round and turned round. Window, bed, door; window, bed, door. And what could she hear her husband saying? His old advice. *Sleep on it*. It could have been a motto on the wall. Don't be rash. Don't rush in. Sort it all out in your head. Line up all the for's and all the against's. Think it through. Don't be *impetuous*.

And it did make sense. Especially when she could easily ask the boy back tomorrow. Then if he still came up to scratch, and her thinking had come out right, she could go ahead and make him the offer. A bed of his own, and a roof over his head, while he found his feet.

What was the opposite of down-and-out? *Up-and-at-'em*? Well, she'd help him to be that. Up-and-at-'em!

Only tomorrow. After one more day—just to be sure.

CHAPTER
NINE

Meanwhile, Nellie fed him well. Not that he ate everything she thrust upon him. But he wouldn't be sleeping on an empty stomach in the hostel that night. She knew that for certain.

And she gave him three pounds, for which he kissed her hand before he put them in three separate pockets.

"Now, listen," she said, suddenly grabbing his own hands. And she stopped. She had a huge lump in her throat and talking was hard. Her eyes had filled up till his face became misty; his eyes more shiny than ever. "If you . . . come back . . . tomorrow. If you . . . want, I've got a hundred little jobs need

doing. And there'll be a chop for dinner. And
. . . ." But she had to stop again. She just
went on clutching his hands and shaking them
up and down the way people do with a
toddler, for a game.

"You come back, eh?" she managed.

"Thank you, ma'am. Thank you, Nellie. I'd
like that fine. Tomorrow."

And with the most delicate touch ever he
leant forward and kissed her on the forehead.
A son's kiss.

"God bless you," he said.

She watched him go, waved to him from
the front door. He seemed to be holding his
head higher. And in spite of his shoes, he
walked, didn't shuffle.

With a sudden surge in her stomach Nellie
nearly called him back. But he'd gone a little
way and she'd have had to shout very loudly
indeed.

She watched him out of sight; then with
one last little look up and down the street —
the one old people always seem to give —

she went inside. She went through into the garden. He hadn't finished up too badly; but she'd give him a few more instructions in the morning. And although she didn't want to, she checked her nick-nacks, her bits and pieces on the little shelves. Of course, everything was in its place.

Eventually, after an evening in front of the television not knowing what she was watching, she went to bed. To sleep not a wink.

CHAPTER
TEN

Lying there in the comfort of her soft bed she stared at the ceiling and thought about William. And straight away she told herself that she'd made a mistake. No doubt about it at all. She had had the good thought. She had known what she wanted to do. But then like someone walking back down the steps from the top board—and she could remember doing that—she had pulled back. She had shown him trust. He hadn't let her down. And she had stopped herself doing what was in her mind to do.

No one who looked at you the way William did, and who kissed you that gently on the forehead, deserved to be down-and-out in

Deptford. Not even for one more night.

The boy could have been tucked up in the little bed right now. Part of a family for the first time in his life, poor little devil—if only for a day or so.

Nellie began to cry silently into her pillow. What wouldn't a mother give to know that a child had a bit of comfort like that?

Cross with herself, disappointed in herself, ashamed of herself, Nellie turned over and faced the wall.

But at least it was only a delay. At least she could make it up to him tomorrow, she thought. And, sniffling a bit, she started saying one of the old prayers.

CHAPTER
ELEVEN

The next morning Nellie was up and about earlier than ever. She washed and dressed, and instead of putting on an overall, she went straight into an afternoon frock.

She went to the spare bedroom and put sheets on the bed, made it up. It needed a new mattress. They'd bought that one cheap, she remembered. It still had Paul's long dent in it. Well, she'd see. A new mattress wouldn't break her, later on.

Meantime, she'd boil a kettle, make a hot water bottle, air it. She put a few books on the wash stand and a bedside light on the card table. She found a folding travel clock. Always like home, she thought, the tick of a clock. A heart sound.

With an excited feeling rising in her stomach she went to the kitchen and forced down some toast. She tried to do this routine job, and that. Until she couldn't resist it any more: and with her cup of tea in her hand she went into the front room to look out on Clipper Street.

Her little wall was empty. It looked bare, even. But there was plenty of time. It was early yet, she knew that.

Miss Fashion Plate ran down the road—in black, with huge padded shoulders. She was eating an apple. Nellie shook her head. They didn't give themselves *time*, some people.

Across the road the boy with the football came banging out of the house. The door was thrown open again and his sister shouted something at him. He made a rude sign and ran off, kicking his football down the street.

Roberta from next door came out: no mother with her today. Nellie watched as the girl made sure she could be seen and waved into the window at her.

"Coo-ee, love." Nellie waved back. But that wasn't the smiling face and the shining eyes she was waiting to see today . . .

The sportsman from over the road ran down to the shop for his paper. She saw him go and she saw him come back, reading.

She saw front doors open and close and cars drive off for the day. She saw British Telecom come to one house, a television and video get carried out of another. As her tea turned cold and pale in her cup she saw people set off shopping and come back home again. And she saw the postman on his second delivery.

Which was when she knew that William wasn't coming. Second delivery, was it? That was dinner time already.

Sadly, Nellie sat down on the hard settee. Well, South London was a very big place, she told herself. Especially to a young Irish boy. He'd forgotten the run of the streets. He was sitting on some other coping somewhere, smelling different flowers. Or he'd had his run of nights at the hostel and moved on out of the district.

Trying to be business-like, she got up and

went back into her kitchen. The two chops she was defrosting were between plates on the table. She left one out and wrapped the other in cling film. It'd do for tomorrow. And, slipping into her overall she went into the garden to tidy the mess William had left.

Boys, boys, boys! she thought. You always have to be behind them. Nice smiles, shining eyes, loving natures—but no sense.

And you never promise them jam to-morrow.

You give it to them today . . . .